CW00493224

Frederick Peterson

Poems and Swedish Translations

Frederick Peterson

Poems and Swedish Translations

Reprint of the original, first published in 1883.

1st Edition 2024 | ISBN: 978-3-38533-157-0

Verlag (Publisher): Outlook Verlag GmbH, Zeilweg 44, 60439 Frankfurt, Deutschland
Vertretungsberechtigt (Authorized to represent): E. Roepke, Zeilweg 44, 60439 Frankfurt, Deutschland
Druck (Print): Books on Demand GmbH, In de Tarpen 42, 22848 Norderstedt, Deutschland

POEMS

AND

SWEDISH TRANSLATIONS

BY

FREDERICK PETERSON, M. D.

"*Except that I have associated for a season with the rose I am the same clay I was before.*"

—GULISTAN OF SAADI.

BUFFALO, N. Y.
PETER PAUL & BRO., PUBLISHERS,
363 MAIN STREET.
1883.

PETER PAUL & BRO., PRINTERS.

TO

AGNES ETHEL

THIS VOLUME IS RESPECTFULLY

DEDICATED.

CONTENTS.

" How the flowers of the aspen-plum flutter and turn! Do I not think of you? But your house is distant.

The Master said, ' It is the want of thought about it. How is it distant?' "

—K'ung Foo-tsze.

TO MY MOTHER.

Through these long months thy love shall bless
  A lonely roamer over seas,
So love me more and sorrow less.

Each tender smile, each past caress—
  How very dear to him are these,
Whom through long years thy love shall bless,

Who to his bosom aye shall press
  The new-found flower of love—heartsease !
So love me more and sorrow less.

To listening Fates each night address
  A low-voiced prayer upon thy knees,
That they long years our love may bless.

Perhaps the pitying Sisters guess
  How Hope the loveless bosom flees :
Love, love me *more*—to sorrow less !

Love shall come back in tenderness,
  Across the months, across the seas,
The steadfast love thy love does bless ;
So love me more and sorrow less.

TO SIGFRIDE.

The sweetest flower that blows
  I give you as we part;
For you it is a rose;
  For me it is my heart.

The fragrance it exales,
  (Ah! if you only knew)
Which but in dying fails,
  It is my love of you.

The sweetest flower that grows
  I give you as we part ;
You think it but a rose ;
  Ah, me ! it is my heart.

SORROW.

She came as queen in robes of gray;
  A doleful chant her maidens sung;
She drove alas! all joy away,
  With her sad eyes and mournful tongue.

"And art thou really Sorrow?" her
  Some sudden fancy made me ask;
She answered not, but I aver,
  She smiled, the rogue, behind her mask!

THE WATER-LILIES.

On slender piles above the river,
  The mansions of the lakemen stand;
The calm, blue waters kiss and quiver;
  The airs bring perfume from the land.

All day the lakemen dreaming lie,
  The fine airs over, waters under,
On golden beds beneath the sky
  Which sunshine makes a golden wonder.

At night-fall close their four green doors,
  Lest some stray moonbeam, dangerous fellow,
Should feast upon the precious stores
  Of perfume and of honey mellow.

All night the lakemen lie in slumbers,
  The too sweet day in sleep forgetting;
The waves chime low in tuneful numbers;
  No memory makes a vain regretting.

Happy the lakemen dreaming so,
  Upon their couches golden-yellow,
With nought of sorrow or of woe—
  Would I were with them, careless fellow!

THE QUEST.

"Where is my body? I cannot find it!
"I have been seeking the wide world over.
"O who could hide it, O who could bind it,
"From me a roamer, a lonely rover?
"Where is my body? I cannot find it!."

When from the earth-life her soul was parted,
It stood in silence and woe and wonder,
And now her spirit seeks broken-hearted
Her body lying the green earth under—
Ah! from her body her soul is parted.

And ever vainly her gentle spirit
Is seeking, seeking the wide world over ;
She loved the earth-life, she would be near it ;
She seeks her body, the lonely rover,
Ah, ever vainly, the gentle spirit !

IN THE ROSE-GARDEN OF SAADI.

A rare old garden this is, Saadi ;
  You made it centuries ago,
  But roses here still bloom and blow,
And souls are called here from the body
  To wander happily to and fro.

A rare old garden, Saadi, this is,
  To walk in when the winds are brusk ;
  These flowers exale an opiate musk
Which soothes the spirit in its blisses
  Afloat upon the purple dusk.

This garden, Saadi, rare and old is;
  Whom can I ask to share its bloom,
  Its damask vapors and perfume,
Its red beds where the sunset's gold is?
  Whom else to share it, Saadi, whom?

THE POEM.

Alas! (how sad a word *alas* is!)
  I would again I were that room in
  So dear because of one dear woman
Whom Memory meets but never passes,
  The chamber her great eyes illumine—
Alas! how sad a word *alas* is!

She was a Poem, a sweet thing created
  By God or some undreamed-of forces,
  Planned ere the suns began their courses,
And in long ages after fated
  To seek again her secret sources—
A gentle Poem, some sweet thing created.

How very sad my soul, alas, is,
  To be again the splendid room in,
  Which those two torches do illumine,
Where Memory halts and never passes
  Because of love of one dear woman,
But kneels remote in shadowy masses !

THE STARS.

From the Swedish of F. M. Franzén.

Little Fanny looked so glad
At the shining stars and said,
" With how many eyes I see
" God look down on me ! "

" God is also still more near,
" Fanny ! see the flowers here.
" Just as God's eyes, flowers thus
" Friendly look on us."

" Mother ! now first clear and fair
" Do I see Him. Know you where ?
" There from out your eyes I see
" God smile down on me ! "

AN UNFORGOTTEN SONG.

One day to me an angel gave
  A melody unknown of men ;
Down in my heart I made a grave—
  The song I buried then.

I did not make the grave so deep,
  But that through many a lonely hour,
Its ghost now haunts me in my sleep,
  With all its mournful power.

The music murmurs in my sleep
  In melody unknown to men ;
I did not make its grave so deep
  But that it comes again.

THE ZOROASTRIAN.

As once perhaps in olden days
  Beneath the far-off Persian skies,
Some reverent one of patient ways
  Did hours before the sun arise
To hasten in the starlit morn
  Up some high hill when winds were cold,
To wait the moment day is born,
  To kneel before the disk of gold;
And when the long rays were descried,
  Which leaped forth from the golden rim
Of that great star he deified,
  To pour out orisons to him—
As may have done this devotee,
  I wake, I wait, I kneel to *thee*.

THE ROBBER.

Quick! see the lawless brigand go
  Around the hill and through the wold,
With pearls and diamonds all aglow
  And all agleam with stolen gold!

Now hidden in the secret woods,
  He hath no longer need to fret,
But softly counts his precious goods—
  The robber is the rivulet.

A MORNING SONG.

The night is gone, the winds renew,
  The stars have vanished one by one;
The flowers lift their cups of dew
  And drink a health unto the sun.

The air is full of orchard blooms,
  And soft the white drifts come and go;
They fill the orchard's ample rooms
  With their sweet-scented summer snow.

I could no longer find my woes,
  Were I to seek them all the day;
They are too deep in summer snows,
  The orchard blooms are in the way.

A HEALTH.

A strange Knight with his visor drawn,
  With gleaming eye and glancing spear,
Sought entrance at the gate at dawn ;
  His princely voice and air austere
  Bespoke both Knight and steed good cheer—
But ere the eve the guest was gone.

Aye, ere the eve came red and brown
  Up from the ocean with the breeze,
The stranger left the coast and town,
  But with the fairest maid of these,
  To cross the gray November seas,
And bind her to his foreign crown.

Deep, deep this bitter cup I drain
  In honor of her gentle eyes,
Her tender mouth that showed no pain,
  Her hair blown under alien skies,
  Of her become the plunderer's prize,
Of her I shall not see again!

CHRISTMAS EVE.

From the Swedish of Runeberg.

The moon shone white upon the down ;
  The hungry lynx cried in the hedge ;
The dog's long howl came from the town,
  When someone walked at the forest edge,
Whose hut lay out upon the wold ;
The Christmas Eve was drear and cold.

He quickened wearily his pace,
  Upon the pathway drifted o'er,
To meet his dear ones' sweet embrace ;
  To them some Christmas bread he bore
Asked at a wealthy farmer's gate—
For they themselves but bark-bread ate.

It darkened more and more, when lo!
 He saw a boy alone and still,
Who sat upon the drifted snow
 And breathed within his fingers chill;
And by the twilight still undimmed
Half-frozen he already seemed.

"Ah, whither goest thou, poor son?
 "Come home with me and warm thee, pray!"
So said, he took the frozen one
 And erelong reached the garden way
Which to his humble cottage led,
His guest with him and loaf of bread.

His wife beside the fireplace sat,
 The youngest child upon her breast.
"You were so long in coming that
 "You must be tired. Come here and rest,
"And you come too!"—so kind, so true,
The stranger to the hearth she drew.

It was not long before her care
  Had made the red flames livelier rise;
Unmindful then herself to spare,
  She took the bread with glad surprise,
And with a bowl of milk in store,
Both forward for the supper bore.

Then quickly from the straw-strewn floor
  Unto the table sparely laid
The happy children went before,
  But by the wall the stranger staid;
Yet kindly she the little guest
Led to a place among the rest.

When now the thankful prayer was said,
  For each a share of bread she broke.—
"*Let blessed be that gift of bread!*"
  So from the bench the strange lad spoke,
And tears his shining eyes forsook
As he the offered portion took.

But when she turned to break again,
  Quite whole had grown the loaf he blessed—
She fixed her eyes in wonder then
  Upon the lad, her little guest,
When still more marvellous than before,
He seemed to be the same no more.

For clear as stars his eyes now gleamed ;
  A halo from his forehead shone ;
A robe, fall'n from his shoulders, seemed
  Like mist upon the breezes blown,
And suddenly an angel, fair
As any in the skies, was there.

Their home was full of blissful light ;
  Each heart with hope and joy was fraught ;
It was an unforgotten night
  Within the good-man's humble cot ;
No feast was fairer or more blest,
Because an angel was their guest.

THE WAYSIDE CRUCIFIX.

A wooden Christ, a wooden cross—
 They mark this still and sacred spot,
Where people pause to pray who pass
 That He forget them not.

The winds are cold and black the skies,
 The rain falls from that drooping face
Like tears, like tears from sorrowing eyes,
 And floods the holy place.

It is a pitying Christ! alas!
  And shall I halt or shall I flee?
O should I pray here as I pass
  That He forget not *me?*

A FANCY.

Some snapping asunder of strings hath bereft us
  Of thy musical laughter so sadder than weeping ;
And some kind of calmness and silence is left us
  By thy marvellous sleeping.

Thy innocent heart it has throbbed into breaking,
  And a trance in thy face makes it paler and colder—
How blest is the fancy there may be a waking
  When the ages are older !

That somewhere away in the barren abysses
  My shadow may meet thine, and mingle in meeting
With sweeter caresses than those of our kisses,
  Which on earth were so fleeting!

That mine may afar in strange regions draw near it,
  Abroad in the cold, in the dim-lighted spaces;
That again and again and again the dark spirit
  It may clasp in embraces!

O Fancy, sweet Fancy, steal, steal away reason,
  And tell me when comes this divorcement from sorrow,
And when shall this bliss be, this heavenly season—
  Tomorrow? Tomorrow.

THE COFFIN OF ST. JULIEN.

Lines in a bottle cast into the sea.

Stranger, in this narrow cell
  Dwelled a soul with love to cheer it ;
Ah, whose was it ? mark it well !
  'Twas St. Julien's gentle spirit.

Sweet and sacred was this saint ;
  Health was his—now ours we term it ;
His own glow our cheeks doth paint—
  Heirs of this immortal hermit.

Lone and old he did much good
  From this cell—O Time endear it !
Now we feel our lives imbued
  With the sparkle of his spirit.

Stranger, hear the praise we sing
  In sad verse, for gods confirm it !
Go—and other votaries bring
  To the Coffin of the Hermit !

THE CORONATION.

Go, Memory, return, you know the way
Along the many paths which have been ours,
Go till you reach the gloomy aisle of firs
That leads up to that little country church,
And lay these flowers upon the grave of her—
Pansies they are which she had loved so much.
And think, O messenger, that where you walk
Once in the old time Death came in to her!
A clear, melodious voice, nor far, nor near,
Nor full, nor faint, nor measurable in tone,
Had read to her the legends on the stones
And died away above the golden hills.
And there before a cavern's marble door,
Smiling she stood, but started suddenly,
For straight she knew upon her temples hung
The tangled poppies and sad cypress crown:
She felt them—drooped her head—and entered in,
Leaving the green day and the sunlit fields.

AT THE GREEN FIR TAVERN.

Down through the windows open wide,
  To fix the noonday on the floor,
The fir-tree's gloomy fingers glide—
  They glide and pause and glide once more.

There sits the round-faced drowsy host!
  Perhaps some song is in his pipe,
Some song to lull, some smoke-like ghost
  Of Bacchus when the grape is ripe.

Without a gray old harper stands,
  And through the noiseless golden noon,
The strings pour forth beneath his hands
  A wailing, sweet Italian tune.

A lonely traveller sits and dreams,
  And dreams have filled his soul anew;
The mountain wine, the music, seems
  To set his sad heart singing too.

For Her the harper strikes the strings;
  The traveller's dream, this song, is Hers;
And loud of Her the throstle sings
  Within the twilight of the firs.

LITTLE KARIN.

A Swedish folk-song.

Once served the little Karin
  Within the young king's hall;
She was a bright star beaming
  Among the maidens small.

Among the maidens beaming,
  She seemed a star aglow;
And once the young king whispered
  To little Karin so:

"And hear thou, little Karin,
"Say, wilt thou now be mine?
"Gray charger and gold saddle—
"These both shall straight be thine."

"Gray charger and gold saddle
"I do not care for—no,
"Give them to thy young queen and
"Let me with honor go!"

"And hear thou, little Karin,
"Say, wilt thou now be mine?
"My reddest crown and golden,
"That also shall be thine."

"Thy reddest crown and golden
"I do not care for—no,
"Give that to thy young queen and
"Let me with honor go!"

" And hear thou, little Karin,
" Say, wilt thou now be mine?
" The half of all my kingdom,
" That also shall be thine."

" The half of all thy kingdom
" I do not care for—no,
" Give that to thy young queen and
" Let me with honor go!"

" And hear thou, little Karin.
" If thou wilt not be mine,
" Then into the spiked barrel
" Shall go that form of thine!"

" If into the spiked barrel
" To put me thou art bent,
" God's angels fair shall see it
" That I am innocent."

So in the spikèd barrel
  They little Karin bound,
And all the king's retainers
  They rolled her round and round.

But then there came from Heaven
  Two white doves fair to see;
They took up little Karin—
  And straightway there were three.

And up from Hell came flying
  Two ravens black to see;
They took the young king with them—
  And straightway there were three.

THE ARROWS.

I am sore wounded ;
I sat in the woodland
  As the moon rosc ;
I arose when the moon did,
And walked in the woodland ;
  How sad the wind blows !

She came when the moon did,
The sweet rose, the fair rose
  Love deifies.
Ah ! I am sore wounded,
By the keen arrows
  That came from her eyes.

TO A SONGSTRESS.

For L. C.

A tone melodious and low
  As we have sometime heard in dreams,
With mellow modulated flow
  Of murmurs under streams,
A tone blithe birds in happy valley,
  On branches swaying to and fro,
  May answer clear and musically.

That tone is thine, and since to me
  It seems as sweet and rare a note
As e'er was plained by bird, or bee
  That singeth in a lily's throat,
Then let these lines faint, far and lowly,
  Speak mutely praises unto thee,
As echoes of their echoes wholly.

But if thy *voice* be sweet and rare
  As tunes of rill and bird and bee,
Thyself art like the lily fair
  Wherein the bee sings gleefully ;
And well do they who feel the power
  Of one dear song of thine declare,
" Yea, thou art like unto a flower ! "

WHAT DYING IS.

To leave the turmoil and the careful tumult,
And wander vaguely to a pleasant region,
Where green fields glow with sheen of summer sunset,
And narrow farther to a sylvan vista,
Whence issue sounds to soothe the spirit's trouble;
To hear the laugh and gurgle of low waters,
And young birds sing with a diviner music,
And young birds carol with a lovelier music,
And evening winds that walk with fainter footfall
Unto the white clouds and the bluer sky-depths;
To rest a little some green willow under,
Whose branches whisper in that shadow-garden,
And hold that hand which hath the tenderest pressure,
And touch sweet lips just as thine eyes are closing:
This is that failing ere the sunset's fading,
This is that dying ere the morn immortal!

To see blue-hooded violets reposing
Among the grasses twining to caress thee
And kiss thy cheek, as if thou wert a sister,
And warm thee with their breath of heavenly odor,
As if thou wert to them indeed a sister;
To find some quiet in the willow vista,
Some little slumber in that shadow-garden:
This is that evening of thy dreamless sleeping,
This is that slumber ere the life immortal!

A gentle waking to a newer beauty,
A gradual unfolding to the soul-life,
As though a rose's chrysalid transported
Into the blooming valley of that Eden;
A slow unfolding of an early blossom;
A little kneeling at the sapphire portals,
And consciousness of all surcease of heartache,
Tumultuous tremor as the soul receiveth
The grander splendor of the spheral chorus,
That joy which "passeth human understanding":
This is that coming of another morning,
This is that morning of the life immortal!

TO LITTLE ROSALIE.

If you were in my garden, maiden,
    The flowers would say:
" This truly is our little sister
    " Of yesterday,
" The one we thought the angels laid in
    " Her dreams away—
" How sweeter, dearer since we missed her!"
    The flowers would say.

They would your tiny form so treasure,
    You could not go,
Your wee, wee feet and hanging tresses
    Entangle so,
That you would lie amidst their pressure
    And sheen and glow
And sweet breath and old-time caresses,
    And could not go.

The trees would look down glad and smiling
    Upon you too ;
The rose-buds would burst quick asunder
    To look at you,
The skies find such blue eyes beguiling
    As lovers do,
And brown bees haunt your mouth in wonder,
    But fear of you.

A BALLAD OF WAR-TIME.

At night upon a lonely road
  A traveller hurries fast,
And who has known his drear abode
  Will look at him aghast !

He comes from distant foreign lands,
  And something strange he bears ;
He holds his own head in his hands,
  And wofully it stares.

A soldier is he, and was slain
  By cruel scimetar,
And long, long years his form has lain
  By high-walled Temesvar.

Each night his home to find he tries,
  Beside the Elbe wave—
In vain ! when dawn is come he lies
  In this same cursèd grave.

Ah, piteous fate, that he who shed
  For love his patriot blood,
Restless and longing, even dead,
  Must lie in hated sod !

At night upon a lonely road
  A traveller hurries fast,
And who has known his drear abode
  Will look at him aghast !

WHY DOES IT SIGH SO HEAVY IN THE FOREST?

From the Swedish of B. E. Malmström.

A little lad is sitting a bleak autumnal even
In quiet playing by a yellow lind;
He sees the lighted windows above him in the Heaven,
And hears the leaves in prattle on the wind;
But while he sits in fancy and many visions sees,
The even of September grows darker in the trees;
Then does it sigh so heavy in the forest.

The little lad he listened, becoming sad in mood,
  Then rose and ran along the path in haste;
He thought dark thoughts of evil that froze his very blood,
  And went astray upon the heather waste;
He thought then of his father, his mother, sisters dear:
"God help me who am little; I would I were not here!"
    Then does it sigh so heavy in the forest.

The moon ascends now softly from out the cloudy rift
  And casts its silver mantle o'er the earth;
The frightened shadows hurry to the mountain bases swift,
  And elfish trolls are flitting to the north;
The mountain summits gleam, but the wildwood it is murk,
And owls pour forth their dirges within the rainy birk;
    Then does it sigh so heavy in the forest.

The little lad then hastened across the moorland wide,
  And thought of many an olden fairy lay,
While night went on and over and stars of Heaven did glide,
  But from his homeward path he went astray.
"Ye gentle stars above me, that move so loftily,
"Ye withered little blossoms, O tell it, tell it me,
    "Who was it sighed so heavy in the forest?'

But all the stars were silent, and little blossoms still,
And many tears of bitterness he shed;
Then came he to an elf-grot, with wingèd swiftness, till
He stood amidst their airy ring and said:
"O ye that move in dances on the heather-growing lea,
"Ye beautiful small sisters, O tell it, tell it me,
"Who was it sighed so heavy in the forest?"

The little queen of elfins now in her smiling way
Caressed the lad upon his rosy cheek:
"Weep not, thou pretty lost one, although so far astray,
"Although so frightened in the woodland bleak,
"But sit here on the greensward of the heather-growing lea,
"And dry thine eyes so tearful and I will tell to thee
"Who was it sighed so heavy in the forest.

"When night descends serenely upon the land and deep,
"And noisy day begins to vanish slow,
"And underneath the green isle the billows go to sleep,
"And all the beauteous stars commence to glow—
"Then mirror-clear and beaming becomes the heavenly dome,
"And hosts of kindly angels beneath it mutely roam
"And weep their silver tears upon the earth.

"Then sees in Heaven's great mirror, poor earth, her form of sin,
"And finds herself a black and spurned abode;
"She reckons up her sins and all murders, lies within,
"Of which a thousand years have formed her load;
"And through her vital marrow death's shudders tremble then,
"Confesses every mountain and prays then every glen,
"Then does it sigh so heavy in the forest."

"Have thanks, thou queen of elfins! I shall forget no more,
"Nor shall I fear my homeward way to go;
"Lo! there the moon beams brightly upon my path before.
"Farewell! we shall not soon forget, I know,
"Each other, and though lowly and very poor I be,
"Yet unto God I promise that never shall for me
"It sigh so heavy in the forest!"

NECKEN.

From the Swedish of E. J. Stagnelius.

Golden clouds at eve are glancing ;
Elves upon the heath are dancing,
And the leave-crowned Necken ever
Rings his harp in the silver river.

Lo ! a lad where trees are sighing,
In the violets' vapor lying,
Hears the sound the waters weave in
Night, and calls through quiet even :

"Poor old minstrel, wherefore chanting?
"Will not sorrows cease their haunting?
"Though thou field and wood enliven
"Still by God thou art not forgiven.

"Paradise's moonlit shadows,
"Eden's flower-crownèd meadows,
"Angels high, whose lights enfold them—
"Will thine eyes no more behold them?"

Tears the old man's face are laving;
Down he dives in the waters waving,
While his harp grows still and never
Sings again in the silver river.

THE PATH.

I leave my home at early day,
  To follow silent through the wood
A crooked, rambling, pleasant way,
  With flowers and birds a multitude.

The rivulet glides by swift and still;
  Loud rondels sings the happy thrush;
But oft I leave him when I will,
  And seek the deeper woodland hush.

Presently it is afternoon ;
  Then from the mountain steal the shades ;
The sun will leave the valley soon,
  And in the mist the pathway fades.

But ah ! can I have lost my way ?
  There is no mark there is no light ;
The path may baffle and betray ;
  Where does it lead to ? It is night.

THE DREAM OF THE HYACINTH.

" Last night the Dream-god made of me
" A mortal maiden, and I lay
" Pale in the grass beneath a tree
" Until a young knight came that way.

" He took me in his arms and said,
" He loved me, I should be his bride ;
" He kissed my lips till they were red
" And called me sweet-breathed, purple-eyed."

So dreams the flower ; its dream is deep ;
  It cannot tell me, but I know ;
How long will these magicians keep
The maid in this unholy sleep
  Before again they let her go ?

AN EXTRAVAGANZA.

After a Nocturne of Chopin.

Have I a lover
Who is noble and free?—
I would he were nobler
Than to love me.
—EMERSON.

Thou art so near me, I do hold thee,
I clasp this clay which thou dost seem of;
Thou art so distant—I enfold thee,
But thou art far from that I dream of.

Below, the river hurries madly—
Thou art so near me, I do hold thee—
The river—ah, I ponder sadly
How I but clasp thee, kiss, enfold thee!

Come, love, come to me and discover
  How I but clasp, enfold and kiss thee;
Thou art so noble, but thy lover,
  He *must* not love thee, *can* not miss thee.

Deep down in this forgetful river,
  Come, love, come with me, I do hold thee—
One moment's pain—my soul forever
  Shall clasp thee, kiss thee and enfold thee.

A DRINKING SONG.

From the Swedish of Bellman.

Drink out thy glass! see, Death is waiting for thee,
  Whetting his sword upon thy threshold here!
Be not afraid! he but the grave before thee
  Opens, then closes haply yet for a year.
Movitz, consumption hangs threatening o'er thee!
    Strike now the octave!
Tune up thy strings and sing of spring and good cheer!

Yellow complexion, thin cheeks faintly blooming,
  Breast sunken in and flattened shoulderblade—
Let's see your hand! each vein, so blue and fuming,
  Seems as if swelled and in moist vapor clad—
Damp are thy hands and their veins stiff as clay now!
    Strike up and play now!
Empty thy bottle, sing and drink and be glad!

WINTER.

Now round the rivulet's castle walls
  Resound no more the summer's praises,
But scarce heard through its frozen halls
  A melody runs in secret places :

For though the wood lies deep with snow
  Which veils from us the mosses' slumbers,
The stream with soft, unceasing flow
  Goes gliding down in golden numbers.

What language speaks the beauteous stream,
  With murmurs under its green apsis,
Unconscious voicings of its dream,
  And music of its gentle lapses ?

Is this but gravity which sings ?
  Or blithe joy in a sense of being,
Or knowledge of more wondrous things,
  And miracles beyond our seeing ?

SNOW.

Some snowflakes fallen from afar,
  Pale, cold, of shining purity,
Seem like unto a beauteous star,
  But they are much more like to thee—
I cannot write how like they are.

The sun may look out any day,
  And they will seek again the skies,
But not till melted quite away
  To drops which sparkle like thine eyes—
Ah, me, if thou wouldst melt as they!

Because so beautiful and far,
  So pale and cold in purity,
I deem them like a lovely star,
  But they are much more like to thee—
Ah, Heaven, how very like they are!

THE SICILIAN TRIAD.

Where are they gone,
  Ah, whither fled,
The songs at dawn?
Where are they gone?
We muse upon
  Their singers dead.
Where are they gone,
  Ah, whither fled?

Sweet sounds they drew
  From heath and hill,
Where soft winds blew—
Sweet sounds they drew,
Grown faint and few
  And almost still;
Sweet sounds they drew
  From heath and hill.

Ah, now no more
  Such songs are sung!
The years of yore
Come now no more,
With their sweet lore
  In sweeter tongue.
Ah, now no more
  Such songs are sung!

HIDE AND SEEK.

Though loitering far, I hear the shout
  Of happy children in their play ;
Some hide and others seek them out—
  How sweet it were to be as they !

Ah ! merrily their voices come
  Across the churchyard green to me ;
God well may bless the distant hum
  Of rosy children in their glee !

Play, little ones, and run and shout
  Among the purple heather blooms!
If some day cares should be about,
Or old, wan Sorrow seek you out—
  Then run and hide among the tombs!

REMORSE.

I saw you once and in that hour
  I wrote a song to last a day,
Which said your body seemed a flower,
  Your soul its fragrance seemed alway.

You thought me bold ; and now I sigh
  Because the sorry rhyme I rue ;
Alas ! a thoughtless wretch was I
  Who dared compare a flower to *you !*

THE CATACOMBS.

Remember ? How one word can stir
  These desolate recesses,
As if a magic word it were
  Which curses or which blesses !

The labyrinth is damp and dark ;
  Here woe, grief, sin are buried ;
Ah, read the lines the torches mark,
  By which the walls are serried !

Up, up into glad day again !
  New hopes the sunlight forges,
While here in darkness, death and pain
  Pale Memory holds her orgies !

THE BLUEBELLS' CHORUS.

Chanson fantastique.

Our carillon will carol on
  In mellow melody
To invisible dead Isabelle
  Who is a bell to be,
When the grass grows green upon her grave
  And swallows follow free,
To cling and swing and sing again
  Upon their trysting tree.

Our carillon will carol on
  In firmer murmur then,
When the grass is green as beryl on
  The new grave in the glen,
When invisible dead Isabelle
  Is made a flower again,
To chime and rhyme all time with us
  And know no more of men.

A RAINY NIGHT.

The night is dark and long winds moan;
  Without the firelight casts no glow;
The rain repeats its undertone
  Unceasingly of woe.

Strange! but it seemed a face looked in,
  So piteously and yet so mild;
Some mother dead it must have been,
  Who seeks her sorrowing child.

" Come to me, grieve no more, ah, stay !
" May I not be belovèd too ?
" I will throw off these robes of clay
" To roam the earth with you."

Then all the window seemed aflame
  From features heavenly, womanly.
" Mother of God, I know thy name—
" Turn not thy face from me ! "

It is a dream—the long winds moan ;
  Without the firelight casts no glow ;
The rain repeats its undertone
  Unceasingly of woe.

IN PRISON.

Dear maid ! put your head to my breast, you will hear
  The prisoner drearily pacing his cell—
What's this ! does he stumble or dream you are near,
  And dreaming you near does he stumble as well ?

For twenty long years in the gloom I have heard
  The prisoner's footsteps—for twenty or more—
Life-sentence it is—and he never has stirred
  From his steady, strong tramp till this hour before !

Dear maid! put your head to my breast, you will hear
  The prisoner knock in the gloom of his cell—
How he strikes on the walls, in his frenzy and fear,
  Lest you go and not hear what he wishes to tell!

ROSES ON THE GRAVE.

From the Swedish of W. von Braun.

Down among the marbles of the churchyard
Thekla went one even with fresh roses
To be laid upon her brother's headstone
As an offering of silent sorrow.
When she slowly came unto the green mound
Where the dear departed lay low-hidden,
Fell she on her knees in sad devotion,
While her prayers flew upward unto Heaven
And her tears fell downward on the velvet.
Then descended Consolation, mild-eyed angel,
To the sisterly and faithful bosom.—
Suddenly disturbed by heavy sighing

Near she saw a low, smooth grave made newly,
And upon that grave a pallid maiden,
Bowed and withered like a frozen lily.
Souls by grief and sadness overburdened
Find in others sweet, enduring friendship,
And her own affliction now forgetting,
Thekla falteringly approached the mourner,
Threw her arms around her softly saying:
"Poor, poor sister, tell me whom thou grievst for!"
The maid was mute but to her *heart* she pointed.
"Poor, poor sister, why art thou so tearless?"
The maid was mute but to her *brow* she pointed.
"On the grave thou hast not any roses;
"Wilt thou not have half of these my flowers?"
Sadly smiling to her *cheeks* she pointed,
To those cheeks so whitely wan and wasted,
And she spoke then in a broken whisper:
"Have I not upon the grave laid roses?"
Then fell Thekla on the poor one's bosom,
And she wept but questioned not thereafter.

NECKROSEN.

From the Swedish of C. W. Böttiger.

A lad leaping down to the ocean strand,
There after a lily extended his hand ;
But God will add unto his angels !

Meanwhile as he stood from the breakers there
A mermaid arose green-mantled and fair.
But God will add unto his angels !

"O bring me the lily which near to thee stands;
"I cannot quite reach it, so little my hands!"
But God will add unto his angels!

The maid plucked the lily for him as he smiled,
But lured him into the waters wild,
For God would add unto his angels!

A WISH.

I fain would be a troubadour
  (If one poor wish be not a sin)
With voice to charm and song to lure,
  And some melodious mandolin.

Then I would sing a song so sweet,
  So strange and low and strong and brave,
That it should pierce beneath my feet
  And thrill you in your quiet grave !

I WILL SLUMBER.

From the Swedish of W. von Braun.

" Darling, in the gentle arms of slumber
" Seek that once thy heart's pain be forgotten,"
Said a hapless mother to her daughter
Who the late departed bridegroom mourned for.
" Only one good friend on earth has sorrow—
" That is night with her sweet peace and quiet.
" Ah ! it is the hours so long and wakeful
" That have paled thy cheeks and dimmed thy glances,
" And my fresh new rose like tempests ravaged.
" Sleep, my poor one ! Dream's befriending angel
" Will give back whom late thou wert forlorn of,
" Whom thou now dost weep, consumed of sorrow.

"Thou, who hast been naught but sweet, O hear me!
"Seek the rest which thou so much hast need of."
Then the daughter breathed, "Yes, I will slumber,
"Seek the rest which I so much have need of.
"Long the night will be. O mother, bless me!
"Kiss me yet again, for I—will—slumber!"
From her mother's breast upon the swansdown
Blest she drooped low, low adown and smiling,
Clasped her soft, white, tender hands together,
Pressing them against her heart with rapture;
Then her eyes even as she sighed closed slowly,
And the mother by vain hope deluded
Stole out gently from the slumberer pallid,
That she might a heartfelt orison offer
Unto Heaven for her sick daughter's slumber.
Yes, she slumbered.
Soon a pitying angel
Gave her back whom late she was forlorn of,
But it was not Dream's—'twas Death's—dear angel.

THE WONDERFUL HARP.

A Swedish folk-song.

There lived a baron beside the sea,
Young is my life !
And two young daughters fine had he.
My heart it is heavy !

The elder was dark as the earth is dun ;
Young is my life !
The younger was white as the shining sun.
My heart it is heavy !

And sister whispered to sister so:
Young is my life!
" Come, let us down to the seashore go!"
My heart it is heavy!

" Though you wash yourself both day and night,
Young is my life!
" You will never like me be clear and white."
My heart it is heavy!

And now as they stood on the shore far from home,
Young is my life!
Pushed the elder her sister down into the foam.
My heart it is heavy!

" O dearest, my sister, help, help me to land,
Young is my life!
" And to thee will I give my red gold-band!"
My heart it is heavy!

"Be sure I shall have thy gold-band red,
Young is my life!
"But God's green earth shalt thou never more tread!"
My heart it is heavy!

"O dearest, my sister, help, help me to land,
Young is my life!
"And to thee will I give my gold-crown grand!"
My heart it is heavy!

"Be sure I shall have thy gold-crown red,
Young is my life!
"But God's green earth shalt thou nevermore tread!"
My heart it is heavy!

"O dearest, my sister, help, help me to land,
Young is my life!
"And to thee will I give my bridegroom's hand!"
My heart it is heavy!

"Be sure I shall soon with thy bridegroom wed,
Young is my life!
"But God's green earth shalt thou nevermore tread!"
My heart it is heavy!

"Greet then my father at home from me;
Young is my life!
"I drink to my bridal deep in the sea."
My heart it is heavy!

"And greet at home my mother so good;
Young is my life!
"I drink to my bridal deep in the flood."
My heart it is heavy!

"Unto my bridegroom greetings take;
Young is my life!
"In the sand my bridal bed I must make."
My heart it is heavy!

There dwelt an old harper down by the shore;
Young is my life!
He saw how the billows a fair form bore.
My heart it is heavy!

He seized the maid where the breakers were,
Young is my life!
And fashioned a beautiful harp of her.
My heart it is heavy!

He took the snow-white breast of the maid,
Young is my life!
That her voice should sound from the harp he made.
My heart it is heavy!

He took the maiden's fingers small,
Young is my life!
Made ivory pins in the harp of all.
My heart it is heavy!

He took the maiden's golden hair,
Young is my life!
And wrought of it harp-strings strange and rare.
My heart it is heavy!

Then he bore the harp to the bridal hall,
Young is my life!
Where desire and joy and pomp ruled all.
My heart it is heavy!

When he struck the harp into melody wild,
Young is my life!
The new bride sat in her chair and smiled.
My heart it is heavy!

At the second stroke which the strings ran through,
Young is my life!
The bridal robes from the bride they drew.
My heart it is heavy!

At the third peal which from the strange harp sped,
Young is my life!
Dead lay the bride in her bridal bed.
My heart it is heavy!

ON THE MOLDAU.

The sun lies red upon the river,
The last glad sun that we shall see,
For night comes soon to part forever,
To part forever you and me.

We have known joy, we have known sorrow,
We have known ah! too much of pain,
But more and more and more tomorrow
Shall come the shadows back again.

The sun lies red above the river,
  The last glad sun that we shall see,
For night comes soon to part forever,
  To part forever you and me.

TO LILI.

Deep in a lonely valley hangs
  A flower so sweet, a flower so pale,
O it were balm for many pangs,
  Could loveliness alone avail!

Its perfumes glide forth on the air
  And hold me in a reverie;
In sooth, dear maid, the flower seems there
  Not thee—but Earth's late dream of thee!

THE LITTLE COLLIER-BOY.

From the Swedish of E. G. Geijer.

" By the kiln in the wood father sits ;
" Mother at home sits spinning.
" Wait, I also shall soon be a man
" And have a sweetheart for the winning.
" It is so dark far, far in the forest.

" Early I started from home with the sun—
" Quicker be, while it does glimmer !
" Unto my father I bring food and drink.
" Soon will the twilight be dimmer.
" It is so dark far, far in the forest.

" I do not fear on the little green path,
" Though I alone in the forest must wander,
" But fir-trees are looking so darkly at me,
" And mountains are casting such long shadows yonder.
" It is so dark far, far in the forest.

" Tra la la ! quick as a bird in its flight,
" Now shall I hurry while humming—
" Oh ! from the mountains it answers so fierce,
" So heavy the words that are coming.
" It is so dark far, far in the forest.

" O were I only with father down there !
" A bear I hear growling and tearing,
" And the bear he is the strongest of men,
" Neither the young nor the old ones sparing !
" It is so dark far, far in the forest.

" The shadow is falling so thick, so thick,
" On the lonely road like a cover ;
" It creeps and it rustles on stone and on stick,
" And trolls in the heather run over !
" It is so dark far, far in the forest.

"O God! there is one—there are two—in their net
"They will take me—ah, see them, how merry!
"They beckon! God pity me, poor little child—
"Now, now for my life I must hurry!
"It is so dark far, far in the forest.

And night it descended, the hour grew late,
And wilder and wilder the shadow;
It crept and it rustled on stone and on stick;
The little one ran to the meadow.
It is so dark far, far in the forest.

With beating heart and with rose-blossom cheek,
By the kiln near his father he fell.
"Be welcome, be welcome, thou dear son of mine!"—
"O I've seen the trolls and much more as well!"
It is so dark far, far in the forest.

"My son, I have sat here so many years,
"And ever God guarded from evil;
"Whoever rightly the "Lord's Prayer" doth read
"Fears neither troll nor the devil,
"Though it is dark far, far in the forest."

THE LAPLANDER'S SONG.

From the Swedish of F. M. Franzén.

Fly, my gentle deer,
  Plain and mountain o'er !
  Soon my maiden's door
Thou mayst paw anear ;
  Rich the mosses grow
  In the drifting snow.

Short indeed the day ;
  The road is very long.
  Hasten with my song !
Let us fly away !
  Here there is no rest ;
  Here but wolves infest.

The Laplander's Song.

Lo, an eagle passed!
  Blest with wings is he.
  Watch yon cloudlet flee!
Were I on it cast,
  I might see the while
  Thee afar to smile.

Thou my heart dost bear,
  Captured hastily,
  As a deer may be
By a kindly snare,
  O thou lurest me
  More than whirling sea!

When I thee have seen,
  A thousand thoughts delight
  Me both day and night—
Thousands though I ween
  They are one alone—
  To take thee for mine own.

Thou mayst hide thee near
  Behind the valley stone,
  Or to the woods alone
Fly with thy reindeer—
  Away, away shall be
  Every stone and tree!

Fly, my gentle deer,
  Plain and mountain o'er!
  Soon my maiden's door
Thou mayst paw anear;
  Rich the mosses grow
  In the drifting snow,

THE CRUSADER.

His loved ones from the turret see
  The knight with lance and shining mail
Who rides away across the lea—
  O Heaven forbid that he should fail !

Long years he fought in Holy Wars
  In the far lands of Palestine,
And now he comes back with his scars,
  To make his glories, dear ones, thine.

Victorious from the Holy Lands,
  He seeks again his native shores ;
Red in the sun his castle stands—
  But weeds have grown before his doors !

ASHES TO ASHES.

Thou tender blossom, more than human,
  Because so fair and pure and humble,
O lovely flower, how could I doom one
  So dear to droop defiled—to crumble
    Like man and woman!

And so, my flower, my love, I swore it,
  That one thing, one, should not so perish,
That mocking Fate should laugh not o'er it,
  Not alway mar what most I cherish,
    While I deplore it.

Now on the white hot coals I place thee,
  Among the ferns of some gone aeon ;
In shining vesture they do grace thee,
  And perfumes as from isles Ægean
    Do soft embrace thee.

No taint, no blemish, naught but ashes—
  Of such fine death thy frame is worthy :
The ermine couch with damask flashes,
  Quick change of heavenly back to earthy,
    No soul abashes.

O bud half-open, thy sweet splendor
  Is risen from the fiery portal,
And atoms, which through stem so slender
  Had crept into a bloom immortal,
    Their work surrender.

CRADLE SONG FOR MY HEART.

From the Swedish of Runeberg.

Sleep, disquieted heart, O sleep !
Worldly sorrow and joy forget !
Let not hope destroy thy slumber,
Nor a dream thy oblivion.

Wherefore dost thou at day look still ?
Tell me, what dost desire from it ?
Haply for thy deeper heart-wounds
Some fair balm-bringing flower ?

Mournful heart, now thine eyelids close;
Daylight's roses thou'st proved enough;
Only slumber's shadow-garden
Hath the herb that will heal thee.

Sleep as lilies that sleep alway
Lightly broken by autumn winds;
Sleep as hind that bleeding sleepeth
With the burden of arrows.

Wherefore pinest for days gone by?
Why remember that blest thou wert?
Sometime must the spring-time vanish,
Sometime joy, O heart, also!

Even thou hast thy May-day seen;
What if lasting it could not be!
Seek not for its tender sunshine
Now in glooms of the winter.

Dost remember the hour's bliss still ?
Greened the forest and trilled the bird,
And the hill with balmy odor
Was the fane of affection.

Dost remember embraces there,
And the heart that had sought for thee ?
Dost remember still the kissed lips
And their dreamy avowals ?

Then when eyes into eyes did look,
Feeling mirrored in feeling lay,
Then, my heart, 'twas time to waken,
Now to slumber forgetful.

Sleep, disquieted heart, O sleep !
Worldly sorrow and joy forget !
Let not hope destroy thy slumber,
Nor a dream thy oblivion.

HAPPINESS.

She smiles and sings the livelong day—
  A very happy maiden she,
Whose blessed fancies charm away
  Her sorrows and her misery!

How sad and strange the people here!
  They sigh and shriek and whisper things
To shun, to loathe, to dread, to fear—
  But all the day she smiles and sings.

Happiness.

'Tis sweet to know that there can be
  Someone whose woe has taken wings—
A very happy creature she
  Who all the day long smiles and sings!

HER SOUL AND BODY.

The wine was in the golden beaker ;
  Its red foam frothed and bubbled up ;
For some fine spirit I was seeker ;
  I found one in that shining cup.

I longed to breathe the sweets it scattered,
  To breathe, to taste, did Fate permit,
But from my lips the cup fell shattered ;
  Then fell and broke my heart with it.

TO ELIN.

The phantoms in my dreams resemble
  The soul of thee ;
They tremble as thy soul did tremble
  From love of me ;
I fain would clasp them in their tremor
  As I clasped thee,
But frightened fly they from the dreamer,
  Like sounds made free ;
Like those sweet sounds the winds are shaking
  From flower and tree,
Which sigh and murmur in awaking
  Melodiously.

To Elin.

Ah, thou dear God, if thou hast power,
  If God thou be,
Restore, restore one gentle hour
  With her to me !

THE BROOK.

All day the noisy brooklet goes
  Among the green hills restlessly,
But soon with gentle silence flows
  Into the bosom of the sea.

Live, restless heart, and throb and think
  All day among the hills with me,
But when the night is come, then sink
  Into oblivion silently.

THE LOST DREAMS.

We came unto an open door;
Pale Dreams with torches went before;
We entered into the sunless cave—
It was the cavern of the grave!

O it was desolate and cold
And wrapped in silence manifold!
The Dreams went far off from my side;
I had such fear I could have died.

Then suddenly the torches' light
Flickered and faded from my sight;
I rushed back through the open door—
The Dreams were lost and came no more!

NORRLAND.

From the Swedish of A. A. Grafström.

HE.

I know a land where silent even beaming
  Attires the heaven dark in northern sheen,
Where under cloudy helms the cliffs grey gleaming
  Guard with ice-cuirasses the low ravine,
Where many a rill from mountains wildly streaming
  Its thunder rolls beyond the distant scene,
Where harps of mermen in the waves are tinkling,
And moon its kisses on the wet harps sprinkling.

Norrland.

SHE.

I know a night as bright as day and tender;
For flowers slumbering the sun shines yet;
And smiling in their youthfulness and splendor,
The Morn and Even are in heaven met;
While waking birds their notes so mournful render,
And all is fragrant as a violet;
There elfins light in swaying circles hover,
Their silver wings the meadow gleaming over.

HE.

I know where forest olden, and the land is,
Where we went under the resounding shore;
I know the sea and where the dim green strand is,
Which round blue ocean its high rampart bore;
A fir-tree nodding there upon the sand is,
Whose bowing head is hung the billows o'er;
There lay our father's house; the bay was by it,
And in this nook the world seemed free and quiet.

SHE.

I know where are the valley and the island,
In flowers and in song-birds rich of yore;

O stands the olden alder on the highland,
  And is our cot still as the cot before,
When in the room I often stood the while, and
  Saw golden sink the sun behind the shore?
Come, reach to me thy true, good hand, my brother,
Return we to that land fair as no other!

IN THE HARZ.

Across the mountain and the valley
  The goat-bells tinkle, tinkle, tinkle ;
The warm winds whisper, sing and dally
  In heather bloom and periwinkle ;

The fir-trees change their gloom for smiling ;
  The long sounds from the distant churches
Float up enchanting and beguiling,
  And lose themselves among the birches ;

In the Harz.

The red-roofed hamlets seem like roses
  Which drowsily the eyes may number,
And far and wide the blue sky closes
  O'er those who dream and those who slumber.

THE PYTHONESS.

Has none thy grace and beauty sung?
  Has no man given thee caresses?
Has no one wish to dwell among
  Thy far-off wildernesses?

Yet thou art delicate and fair,
  Thou art so graceful and so slender;
Canst thou not charm into thy lair,
  Or trust and love engender?

How bright and strange and strong thine eyes,
  Deceiving, luring and disarming !
'Tis good that most of us are wise
  Beyond thy might of harming !

THY BOUQUET.

The lily of the valley lent
  Its odor of green solitude;
It seemed a lowly monument
  Of some sweet sorrow in thy mood.

The modest violet repined
  I know, to leave its forest dell,
And yet it yielded undefined
  Remembrances of one loved well.

Thy Bouquet.

I knew not if it were dear hopes
  That I might look upon them soon,
But the rose unveiled the golden slopes
  With birds and rivers in the noon.

O lily, violet and rose,
  Conveyers of some secret thought,
Your message still completer grows
  Since with you blooms forget-me-not!

BETWEEN THE TWILIGHT AND THE DAWN.

Between the twilight and the dawn,
  While slumber holds my limbs and senses,
Save the slow breathing, life is gone
  And left to sleep her slight defenses.

How still my body, ah, how quiet,
  Between the twilight and the dawn !
How much more mad my fancies riot
  Because it sleeps in silence on !

How much more mad, how much more wild,
  How much more fanciful my soul is !
It roams thy room, my happy child,
  Entranced among thy holy holies.

And, oh, if it do bend so near,
  That thy too tremulous lips it brushes,
Yet have no fear, in dreams no fear,
  But sleep on in unbroken hushes.

To some sweet place my soul is gone,
  While slumber holds my limbs and senses,
Between the twilight and the dawn—
  O Death destroy their frail defenses
And let them moveless slumber on !

EBBA AF HJELMSÄTER.

Full many things were dear in earth,
  Sadness and loveliness, my thrall,
But you were dearer, you had worth
  Beyond them all.

I leaned above your gentle face
  Seeing no sorrow and no pain,
And now all night my wild thoughts chase
  You through my brain.

THE DEATH OF HOPE.

My lady lay all listlessly,
With the doomed day about to die,
And did her lips in moving pray?
'Twas thus my lady lay.

Her eyes were full of sombre light,
As if she knew of nearing night
And gazed upon an unknown way—
'Twas thus my lady lay.

The Death of Hope.

Half rising heavily on her hand,
She looked a long look o'er the land
Growing with gloaming into gray—
Then low my lady lay.

A soft sob and a softer sigh,
As of leaves that stir when winds pass by;
Be meek and mourn as mourn I may,
For low my lady lay.

WITH A WATER-LILY.

From the Norwegian of H. Ibsen.

My loved one, what I bring, ah, see !
A flower with snowy wings to thee ;
Upon the still stream slumbering
Dream-heavy swam it in the spring.

If thou wilt place it where 'tis meet,
Then place it on thy bosom, sweet ;
Behind its petals secretly
A deep and silent wave will be.

With a Water-lily.

Beware, my child, the gliding stream!
Dangerous, dangerous there to dream—
For Necken sounds his lute asleep—
The lilies lie above it deep.

My child, thy bosom is the stream.
Dangerous, dangerous there to dream!
The lilies lie above it deep—
And Necken plays although asleep.

THE FLAME IN THE WIND.

It starts and shivers, pales and trembles,
  Now fixed and certain, now despairing;
Now thin, it some wan ghost resembles,
  Once bright and beaming and uncaring.

And now, behold it leap and quiver,
  With its last strength, but fade in trying!
Thus I start, tremble, pale and shiver,
  Now fixed and certain and now dying!

THE BELL.

The body is a temple
  As men have said ;
My heart is a bell
  Which tolls love dead.

Love lies in the transept
  All clothèd in white ;
Through the windows low
  Comes the wan red light.

Past days come slowly
  To look at her,
And they sigh as they think
  What her glories were.

The body is a temple
  As men have said ;
The heart is a bell ;
  It tolls love dead.

THE MUMMY.

I laid her memory away
  With one sweet rose that she had given,
Here in a secret drawer one day—
  No record has that day in Heaven.

And many soulless years have died
  Ere happy chance again reveals it,
All bandaged, rolled and swathed and tied
  In one long ribbon which conceals it.

The Mummy.

Unrolled, but fragrant dust I stir,
  Yet *she* is there as love once showed her—
For the dead rose in its sepulchre
  Embalmed the maiden with its odor.

TO MUSIC.

Late thou spokest to me,
  Giving wings to my thought,
For my soul was made free
By thy sweet mystery,
  But again it is caught.

But where did it go?
  Why came it again?
Ah ! I feel the sad blow
The awaking to know—
  Ah ! I feel the sad pain.

To Music.

Late thou spokest to me,
   Waking dreams in my thought,
For my soul was made free
By thy strange mystery,
   But again it is caught.

TO THE SILENT KING.

O thou austere and silent king,
  No more my fancies do forswear thee,
But to thy shadowy shrine they bring
  This token of the love I bear thee.

Though whom thy sad and fatal eyes
  Do fix upon must fail and falter,
Though whom they see—tomorrow dies—
  I hang these verses at thy altar.

I hang them at thy shrine, O king,
  Amidst the moaning and the sighing !
From hate I turn to worshipping,
  And unto loving from defying.

If that God be as mortals say,
  Who changes what seems sweet to curses,
Then bids us kneel to Him and pray—
  I turn from Him to ask thy mercies.

Or if, as fewer men conceive,
  All soul is due to dust's endeavor
Its lowly form and place to leave—
  How much more am I thine forever !

For, after all, to him who fails,
  Whom thy stern eyes so wear and wither,
Thy fatal look so blights and pales,
  Thy influence draws unswerving hither,

Thou grantest this: that he shall sleep
  Through all these centuries' uproar listless,
In earth's great tumult silence keep—
  A sweet oblivion and resistless.

Ah! him thy beauteous eyes shall hold
  Till grief is gone and past is passion;
Then shalt thou to thy bosom fold
  Him dreamless in thy pitying fashion.

So, Wearer of the Cypress Crown,
  Thou sombre liege of my adoring,
Here at thy feet I lay me down,
  Thy mercy and thy aid imploring:

That thou wilt erelong deign to lay
  Upon my head thy hand forgetful,
So soothing all these shapes away
  Which haunt me in this fever fretful;

Till care and weariness shall cease
  For me within these shadows kneeling,
And I shall feel thy blissful peace,
  Thy drowsy languor through me stealing ;

And thou shalt hold me with thine eyes,
  No more this bitterness deploring,
Through all these noisy centuries,
  Thou silent God of my adoring !

AXEL.

FROM THE SWEDISH OF

ESAIAS TEGNÉR.

"His willing Muse on hills of Sweden strayed,
Though far too queenly for a land so lone,
For lofty was she, as some Northern maid,
And all sweet hues of Southron seemed her own;
Sometimes but fair as Grecian goddesses,
Sometimes a glory in the robe of morn,
Now Axel's maid in passion's tenderness,
Now Frithiof's bride whom milder loves adorn."

—MALMSTRÖM.

AXEL.

The olden time is dear to me,
The Carolinian era[1] olden,
For it was glad as conscience golden
And valorous as victory ;
While still upon the Norland lies
Its halo round encircling skies,
And mighty forms of heroes true,
With yellow belts and coats of blue,
At twilight wander far and near.
I look with awe as ye appear,
O heroes, who on high abide,
With kirtles, and long swords at side !

An agèd warrior I knew in
The dear days of my childhood, when
On earth he stood, but even then
An arch of victory in ruin.
And from his century brow there shone
The only silver which he had,
And scars upon his forehead said
What runes say on a bauta-stone.[2]
Himself a poor man, he had felt
The poor man's lot, but scorned its pain ;
While in a forest hut he dwelt,
His soul still sought the battle plain.
But two bright jewels were his care
Whose worth the world had not outweighed—
His Bible and the ancient blade
With " Karl the Twelfth " engraven there.
The battles by that chieftain fought,
Now in a hundred writings sought,
(That eagle flew so far around)
Were in the old man's memory stored,
Like urns of warriors deplored
Within some green old burial mound.
O when he spake of danger near
The monarch or his men in blue,

How high he held his head anew,
How glowing did his eyes appear,
How sturdy as a sabre's clang
Each word that from his two lips sprang !
So oft and long at night he sat
And talked of former time and fame ;
Whene'er he spake his monarch's name
He lifted off his threadbare hat.
I stood in wonder by his knees,
(For then I reached but little higher)—
The high-born image of his sire,
Which youth then saw, my manhood sees,
And many a legend undefined
Dwelled afterward within my mind
Sword-lily-like, whose embryo
Doth slumber under winter snow.

The old man rests and is no more.
Peace to his dust ! This story's worth
I owe to him. O take it, North,
And Axel's fate with me deplore !
Beside his tale my song is nought
But simple rhymes together brought.

In Bender[3] lay the mighty king,
His country waste with pillaging,
His name, late honored, laughed to scorn.
His followers, like a chief forlorn
Who late the deathly chill has felt,
Behind their lifted bucklers knelt,
And now no hope of succor blessed
Another than his noble breast.
Though battle was the pages turning
Of Fate's book, though the earth did sway,
Serene stood he like some archway
Unharmed within a city burning,
Some cliff above the wild sea-wave,
Or Fortitude beside the grave.

One evening unto Axel said he,
" Here is a note "—a message laid he
Within his hands—" Haste thou away,
" And, Axel, ride both night and day
" Up unto Sweden ; when dost land,
" Commit this to the Council's hand.
" But hence with God this evening fare
" And greet for me the mountains there ! "—

Young Axel, loving well to ride,
With joy received and sewed it in
His girdle. Under Holofzin[4]
His father fell the king beside,
And left alone the army's son
Grew up in din of sword and gun.
His was a form of beauty, and
Such as e'en now the North may bear,
As fresh as rose, but tall and fair
As any pine in Sweden's land.
As heaven upon a cloudless day
His brow was arched and bold and bright,
And serious in their earnest light
His noble features ever lay.
You saw it in his shining eyes,
That they were made to look above
With honest hope and trusting love
To the Father of Light within the skies,
And down with fearlessness on him
Who sees alone the midnight dim.—
Among the royal guards[5] he found
A place with souls like his renowned,
A little band whose number small
Was one for every Dipper star,
Or nine, as Memory's daughters are,
And wisely were they chosen all.

They proved themselves by sword and flame ;
It was a christened Viking-stem,
Not unlike that preceding them,
Whose dragon-ships through ocean came.
They never slept upon a bed,
But in their cloaks upon the earth
'Mid drifts and tempests from the north
As calmly as where flowers spread ;
They oft crushed horse-shoes in their games ;
None ever saw them round the flames
That crackle in the fire-place bright ;
They rather chose the warmth of balls
As red as the round sun which falls
Slow down in blood some winter night.
It was their law in battle bold
That one should yield to seven first,
With breast still turned unto the worst—
The back no victor should behold.
And lastly was a charge beside,
Most arduous duty yet assigned—
Unto no maid to turn their mind
Till Karl himself had found a bride :
However blue two eyes might beam,
However red two lips might be,
However fair some bosom seem,
Like swans upon a gentle sea,—

To close their eyes—or haste away,
For wedded to their swords were they.

Young Axel mounts his charger gay
And gallops swiftly night and day
Until he comes to Ukraine's streams,
When suddenly the woodland gleams
With ambushed sabres bright around,
And now a circle guards the ground.
"Thou bearest from Bender Karl's decree—
"Dismount, surrender it to me!
"Dismount or die!"—his sword held high
Comes down in Swedish plain reply;
The speaker humbled by his worth
Bows low in blood unto the earth.
Beside an oak in bold affray
The warrior playeth now his play;
Where'er the heavy sabre sings,
It bends a knee and red blood brings;
He keeps his covenant aright;
Not one to seven—that were small—
His sword on twenty swords does fall!
He fights as did Rolf Krakè fight[6]—
In his distress no aid asks he,
But only seeks death's company.

Yet wounds with mouths of purple hue
Now whisper his last moments too ;
Though round his heart the blood grows chill,
His fingers grasp the weapon still ;
But darkness fills his eyes, and white
He sinks into the long, long night.

But hark ! the woods give forth a sound,
And falcon bold and faithful hound
Follow the prey. In hurried chase
A company swings up apace.
Upon a spotted steed advances,
With habit green and cheeks rose-red,
With speed as if by whirlwind led,
An Amazon fair as daylight's glances.
In fright the band of robbers flies.
As from the dead her courser shies,
With one quick spring she leaps to earth
And sees him lie, as in the glen
The oak lies fallen on bushes when
The storm has ravaged from the north.
How fair he lay there in his blood !
Maria bending o'er him stood
Like Dian who, in years before
Descending from the heavenly door

To Latmos, far from hunting flown,
Leaned over her Endymion ;
But he who spells on Dian cast
Was not more beauteous than this last.
A spark of life is still descried
Within his bosom bare and torn,
And on a bier of branches borne,
Which but a moment does provide,
The pallid one they quickly bring
Unto her dwelling neighboring.

Beside his pillowed head she sate,
Her pity and sad grief prevailing,
And fastened on his features paling
Her glances worth a king's estate.
She sat as in the groves of Greece,
(Fair land which time now overthrows !)
A wild flower often lonely grows
Beside a fallen Hercules.
At length from trance awakened weak,
He starts up and begins to speak,
But, ah, his eyes before so mild
Now stare around him vague and wild :

" Where am I? Girl, what wilt from me?
" Me never must a woman see!
" I unto Karl the king am bound.
" Thy tears must fall not in my wound.
" My father in the Milky Way
" Is angered, he has heard my vow.
" How fair though is the tempter now!
" How luring! Dark one, do not stay!
" Where is my girdle! where my note
" Which Karl himself my ruler wrote?
" My father's sword is good—it bites
" Right faithfully the Muscovites.
" It was a pleasure thus to slay—
" If but the king had seen the fray!
" They fell like grain before the steel—
" I almost seemed myself to reel.
" The letter I to Stockholm take,
" For it my honor is at stake.
" Up! moments now are dear to me!"—
Thus speaks in raging fever he,
But paly sinks the warrior then
On peaceful pillow down again.

Both life and death sought mastery,
But life its forces brought anew

Till death and danger slow withdrew ;
Well now indeed could Axel see
With clearer eyes though weak and dim
The angel sitting near to him.
Unlike was she idyllic maids
Who go and sigh in greening glades
And pine for aye in one same spot,
With golden hair like sun just set,
Each cheek a pink night-violet,
Each eye a blue forget-me-not.
An Eastern child was she ; as fair
Upon her lay her raven hair
As midnight on some rose-clad field,
And joy's glad mood, the only truth,
Sat proudly on her brow of youth
Like Victory graven on a shield.
Her face was fresh as limners trace
Aurora's with its crown of grace,
And she had become an Oread,
As light of foot, as gay and glad,
And high her bosom's billows came
By youthfulness and vigor heaved ;
Her form the rose and lily weaved,
Her soul was purest fire and flame—
A southern summer sky, most fair
With golden sun and perfume rare.

There struggled in her twilight eye
A heavenly and an earthly brand ;
At times she glanced up proudly, and
Seemed like the bird of Jove on high,
And sometimes mildly as the two
Doves that the car of Venus drew.

O Axel, soon thy wounds' deep smart
Is over and but scars remain ;
Outside thy breast will heal again,
But, ah, how is it with thy heart ?
Look not so fondly on that hand
Which ever answered pain's command—
That hand like marble white and fine,
It must not linger long in thine ;
It is more perilous by far
Than at the siege of Bender, where
Hard hands of Ottomans there were
With pistol and with scimetar ;—
Those rosy lips that bloom anew
And only part to murmur through
A spirit-song of hope and cheer—
Far better if again were heard
The thunder that Czar Peter stirred
At Pultowa in a former year.

And when about in summer warm
Thou falterest all pale and wan,
Then, Axel, lean thy sword upon,
And not upon that rounded arm,
Which Amor moulded thus it seems
As downy pillow for sweet dreams.

O Love, thou earth and heaven wonder,
Thou inspiration blest and rare,
Like godlier and fresher air
Life's suffocating forest under!
Thou heart in Nature's bosom calm!
Thou both to man and God a balm!
The drop the drop seeks in the sea,
And all the heavenly stars we see
In bridal-dance from pole to pole
Around a common centre roll.
In human souls thou dwellest frail,
A twilight gleam, a memory pale
Of fairer and of better days,
When thou wert at thy childhood plays
In heaven, whose great pavilion blue
Thou sleptst in after frolic warm
Each evening on thy Father's arm.

Thy riches were by knowledge given ;
Thy speech was but a gentle prayer ;
And unto thee dear brothers were
All winged and beauteous sons of heaven.
But, ah, thou'st fall'n down here, since when
Thy love is not as pure again.
Still 'mong beloved one comprehends
The nearness of thy heavenly friends,
And hears their voices in the song
Of spring, or tunes of bard among.
Once more thy soul is gladdened then,
As his who hears in wanderings
A song of fatherland which brings
His Alps and boyhood back again.

It was at night. The Even lay
Upon her western bed in dreaming,
And silent, priests Egyptian seeming,
The stars began their march away.
And Earth seemed in the starlight pale
A happy bride who standeth fair,
A crown upon her raven hair,
And smile and blush beneath her veil.

While from the day's long play at rest,
Still lay the Naiad laughing low,
And reddening sunset all aglow
Seemed like a rose upon her breast;
Then every Cupid who lay bound
When shone the sun was free to ride
On all the moonbeams far and wide,
With dart and bow the grove around—
The grove, that dim and green arcade
Where Spring her recent entrance made.
Among the oaks the nightingale
A melody caroled through the dale,
As tender and as pure and plain
As any poem of Franzén.[8]
It seemed that Nature now was glad
That she a silent moment had,
So full of life and yet so still
One might have heard her pulse's thrill.—
Then slowly walked together there,
With minds entranced, the youthful pair;
As lovers rings exchange, so they
Their memories of childhood's day.
Of happy long gone days he told,
Passed in his mother's cottage old,
Built up of fir-wood painted red
And hidden in the forest grand;

And of his cherished fatherland
And courtly kinsmen who were dead.
He told how oftentimes and long
The deep and olden warrior-song
And leather-bound historic lore
Awoke his soul to rise and soar ;
And how in many a dream at night
A man of steel he sat upright
Upon the twelve-foot pacer Grane,[9]
And rode like Sigurd Fofnisbane
The fires that were enchanted through
To Brynhild fair, whose mountain tower
Stood flaming in the moonlight hour
Above the bays that round it grew.
Within his chamber ill at ease,
He fled among the greenwood trees
And climbed with boyish pleasure up
To the eagle in the fir-tree top,
And swung upon the northwind slow
With heart refreshed and cheek aglow.
O could one but a ride obtain
Upon the passing cloudlet's wain,
And far beyond the harbor glide
Into the world so fair and wide,
Where victory nods and glories wait
To wreathe the hair of brave and great,

Where Karl the king (who it appears
Is older by some seven years)
With good sword plucks what crowns he may,
Then godlike gives them quick away !
" My mother after fifteen years
" No more embraced me, and with tears
" I hastened thence to Poland o'er.
" To camp since then my life has turned,
" And faithful as a watch-fire burned
" In clash of steel and cannon roar.
" But sometimes saw I birds meseems
" That fed with soft caress their young,
" Sometimes a child that played among
" The flowers on the brinks of streams ;
" Then vain became the battle's thunder,
" And those sweet scenes and places grew
" Into my soul with golden hue
" Of happy children green groves under ;
" And by a quiet cottage door,
" A maiden stood, and sunset's flame
" Lit up her face which was the same
" I saw at times in dreams before ;
" But now in sooth these forms appear
" Forever in my soul to be ;
" I close my eyes and still I see
" Them all around alive and clear.

" The maid who stands among them, she
" Is thine own mirrored self, Marie ! "

Then timidly replied Marie :
" What pleasure does not man possess !
" The stronger one is fetterless
" And was from birth among the free ;
" And danger's charm and glory's name
" And earth and heaven—all his became.
" 'Twas woman's fate to have been made
" To be through life to man an aid,
" A solace to his poignant grief
" Forgotten when he finds relief ;
" The offering she, and he the fire
" Which unto heaven doth bright aspire.—
" Beneath the Czar my father fell ;
" I scarce recall my mother's face ;
" The moorland child grew wild apace
" Upon these lands, where slaves serve well
" Their master's whims, bear cheerily
" The idol of their misery.
" A noble mind must loathe to stay
" With those who every nod obey.
" Didst see upon the moorland wide
" The fiery steeds that there abide ?

" As brave as hero, light as hind,
" They yield them to no lord's command ;
" With ears erect they steady stand
" And, turned to danger, face the wind,
" When sudden in a cloud again
" The throng sweeps swiftly o'er the plain
" With unshod hoof to fight their foes ;
" And they too have their joys and woes.
" Ye children of the desert fair,
" How blest your life on meadows there !
" Full oft I called and bade them bide,
" Whene'er my neighing Tartar steed,
" Like bridled slave me bore with speed
" To his unshackled brothers' side ;
" They would not heed my words nor stay,
" But fled disdainfully away.
" Oppressive to my soul unbound
" Became the castle's irksome round,
" And warfare I with zeal incurred
" With forest wolf and mountain bird,
" And oft from bears' paws did reclaim
" A life which then of worth became.
" But, Nature, none can change thy will !
" Within a cottage, on a throne,
" A housewife or an Amazon,
" A woman is a woman still,

" A vine which unsupported dies,
" A being partly incomplete
" Whose life unshared is life unsweet,
" Whose joy in twofold pleasure lies,
" There throbs within my inmost breast
" A feeling of a sweet unrest,
" A longing I can ill define,
" Such pain and yet such bliss is mine.
" It has no bound, it has no aim,
" It is as if I winged became
" And went from earth and all that mars
" To God's pure mansion and the stars,
" As if again I downward fell
" Unto those beings cherished well—
" The trees whose growth with me was made,
" The hill in flowery crown arrayed,
" The river running with love-chimes—
" I heard them, saw a thousand times
" But with a statue's unconcern—
" Now first, now first my love they learn !
" It is for self my love is weak;
" It is a feeling far more true
" And loftier than before——" Here flew
A blush across the maiden's cheek,
And meanings which she could not say
Within a sigh were breathed away.

Now sings the nightingale in gloom;
The moon in clouds to listen is,
And with a long, eternal kiss,
As warm as life, as true as tomb,
Their spirits mingle in one tone,
One blissful harmony alone.
They kissed as in an altar-fire
Two flames oft kiss and then unite,
And flash aloft their higher light,
And nearer unto heaven aspire.
For them the earth-life was no more,
And time stood still which fled before;
For every moment in the rounds
Of time is measured and has bounds,
But Death's cold kiss and Love's embrace
Are children of a deathless race.
O happy ones! If earth and all
Should change to mist, they would not see;
If heaven should now in ruin be,
They scarcely would perceive its fall:
Like guardian souls of South and North,
With heart to heart they would remain,
Unconscious that they did attain
To bliss of heaven from that of earth.

Back from the heavenly journey made

First Axel came: " Now, by my blade,
" By Northern faith, by stars of night
" Which stand like bridesmaids clothed in white
" And through the midmost forest shine,
" By earth and heaven, thou now art mine!
" O were I far from battle's riot,
" In some kind dale where peace and quiet
" Between the mountains ever lie,
" With thee to live, with thee to die!
" But, ah, an oath, an oath between,
" With warning look and pallid mien,
" Comes silent and lays fingers chill
" Upon our bosoms fervid still!
" But fear not! Time a change will make
" And loose the oath I dare not break.
" I must away! When May next year
" Invites us to her floral cheer,
" Once more I'll come, whate'er betide,
" To claim thee as my wife, my bride.
" Farewell, my soul, we meet again,
" Farewell, a long farewell, till then!"

So said he turned, and in his hands
He took his belt, he took his blade,
And fearlessly his journey made

Over the Czar's one hundred lands.
The wood his cover made by day ;
By night the warrior held his way
Toward that heavenly centre far,
Our Northern never-changing star,
Toward the Wain of Charles the bold,
Which never wanders from our sight,
That Wain with pole all burnished bright
And wheel-spikes fashioned out of gold.
So riding through a thousand woes
Amidst a multitude of foes,
He came to Sweden's capital
Where all his strange adventures hear,
And brought the message and good cheer
As Karl bade to the Council hall.

But meanwhile, in her vacant halls,
Maria sighs brave Axel's name ;
Deep in the wood she sighs the same
And teaches mount and vale her calls :
" What oath restrains him with its band ?
" Some maiden in his fatherland,
" An older flame? He loved before ?
" Alas ! my heart distrusts the more.
" Thou maid, by Northern snows concealed,

" Soon one of us to fate must yield !
" Thou knowest not what burns in me ;
" Far, far beyond thy frozen sea,
" And far beyond thy mountains high,
" I will pursue thee—thou must die !
" Yet—Axel left the North in youth
" And has not been there since in truth,
" And distant from the din of fray
" It is the shy Loves' wont to stay.
" 'Tis honor, not a faithless art,
" Upon his open forehead lies ;
" It is in glances of his eyes
" I see the bottom of his heart,
" As day beholds the firm bed through
" Some river clear and silver-blue.
" Why flyest thou ? Thy oath enslaves
" Thee, and for what ? This breast to tear ?
" What—but my voice dies into air
" Like sighs of widow by her graves,
" Like plaining of a dove which flies
" Unanswered round the earth and skies.
" Between us roar the sea and wood,
" And, ah, he cannot hear my woe.
" What if I follow him ? But, no,
" That ill becomes my womanhood.
" A woman ? Who will know ? A blade

" I bear, the man is soon arrayed.
" Great dangers have I often hailed,
" When life or death was chance indeed ;
" Fixed have I grown upon my steed,
" And never has my weapon failed.
" Some god has made me this design—
" Now Axel, Axel, art thou mine !
" I seek thee in the farthest North,
" I seek the round the whole of earth,
" From dale to dale, from strand to strand
" This secret from thy lips to wring ;
" Take me, O War, upon thy wing
" And set me down in Axel's land ! "

So said so done. To say and do
Are one with woman. Garments new
She donned. In hat that warriors wear
She hid the dark night of her hair,
Concealed her bosom in disguise,
And filled a knapsack with supplies,
While from her shoulder soft and fine
Was hung the deadly carabine.
Within that zone Greek legends sing
A crooked sword was glimmering;
Then round about her lips she drew

A shadow like a beard unshorn—
It was as if one should adorn
With mourning crape sweet roses two.
She seemed in sword and belt's device
Like Amor in a hero's guise
Whom Clinias' son once bore embossed
Upon his buckler brightly glossed.

"Farewell, thou home serene and mild!
"Sometime with love when reconciled
"I shall return to thee once more.
"No longer must I stay my flight!
"Take me within thy shade, O night,
"And to my heart's friend me restore!"—
E'en then upon his conquered field
Within the Norland's sleeping eye,
Stood Peter's capital whereby
Earth's mortgaged crowns he now makes yield.
It then was petty. In the bay
It like a new-born dragon lay.
Its nature entered it while young,
When on the sunny shingle coiled;
Soon in its tooth the poison boiled
And soon it hissed with cloven tongue!

'Tis there prepared for Sweden's strand
Lies many a ship with blade and brand,
And thither makes Maria way;
Amidst bright swords and banners gay
She presses forward to entreat
A place aboard the northern fleet.
The chieftain of the fiery hordes
Surveys her keenly with these words:
"More dangerous must thou be when
"The maidens see thee, than when men.
"When thou art sent against them they
"Will scarcely pull thy beard away.
"Still thou wilt ways of war be taught
"By those who in the battles fought
"Seek life or death. But o'er each land
"St. Nicholas and God command."

Now swell the sails and swift keels plough
The foam upon the eastern bay,
And soon in sunset's fiery ray
Stand Sweden's cliffs, appearing now,
Where time and ocean long have rolled,
Like Nature's giant-buoys of old.
They disembarked at Sotaskär,[10]

A spot to true hearts dear and fair,
Where parted once forevermore
Sweet Ingeborg and Hjalmar chief,
Where afterward she died of grief
And he to Odin wandered o'er;
And there her ghost is sitting still
Lamenting him upon the hill.
Thou northern Leucas, soon will perish
Thy name in days of legends known,
But Hjalmar's death-song will atone
And thee the hearts of poets cherish!

Already burn the hamlets nigh,
And children shriek and women fly—
They know too well the Russian blood;
The bells ring round the neighborhood
To tell their course, all night, all day,
But, ah, the dead cannot awaken—
O woe, thou poor land, thou forsaken,
Within their graves thy warriors stay!
Still danger to their land could call
Together lads and old men, all
With swords once used on German ground
Beneath great Gustaf Adolf's banner,

And halberds in the self-same manner
Used when they crossed the Danish sound,
Then here and there an arquebuse
With rusty lock and lighted fuse.
These were the men who then arose,
A little band and poorly armed,
Unhesitating, unalarmed,
To march against their many foes.
But not as man with man they fight,
Since hangs a cloud upon the height,
And foemen from their mountain-hold,
Whose lines undaunted none can flank,
Strike death in volleys quick and bold
Upon their thinned, revengeless rank.

As comes great Thor full angrily
With hammer and with girdle round,
So Axel comes upon the ground
Where flight and terror seem to be,
A helping angel sent for weal,
Whose arm is death, whose bosom steel;
Now here, now there, he guides the fight
Alert upon his charger white.
"Stand, Swedes, and close your lines anew!

" King Karl hat sent me here to you,
" And greets his loyal men through me.
" Let 'God and Karl' the war-cry be!"
" God and King Karl!" the cry goes round;
They hear the brave one's voice resound.
The cliff, whence death strikes all who climb,
Is stormed within a moment's time;
They close the yawning gullies soon,
While arms and corpses round are strewn,
And blind but true the broadswords beat
Upon long ranks in wild retreat,
For startled flies the robber-band
To drag the cables from the strand.

Like sated beast of prey is seen
Still Slaughter sleeping on the lea;
The moon pours from the canopy
Upon the horrid field her sheen.
Along the bay in shadows lying,
Among the dead, walks Axel sighing.
They lie together face to face.
How close and rigid their embrace!
Wouldst thou a faithful clasp behold?
Look not on Love's where they enfold

Each other smiling tenderly ;
Go to the battlefield and see
How Hate beneath the deadly smart
His foeman presses to his heart !
Ah, fly the joys of love and cheer
Like sighing winds in early year,
But hate, necessity and grief
Are steadfast until death's relief.
So sighing, suddenly a cry,
A moan in night breaks on his ear :
" O Axel, bring me water here,
" And take my farewell ere I die ! "
At words like these, such well-known sounds,
Among the rocks he headlong bounds
And sees—a youth who leans unknown
Wounded and bleeding on a stone.
The moon from clouds peers forth and seeks
Her pallid face—then shudders he
And in a tone of horror shrieks,
" O blessed Jesu, it is she ! "

Ah, she it was ! With hidden smart
She whispers to him soft and light,
" Good even, Axel, no, good night,
" For Death is sitting by my heart.
" What brought me here, O ask not me !

" It was my blinded love of thee.
" Ah, when the day to darkness wears,
" And men stand by the grave's new door,
" How changed from what they seemed before
" Are life and all its petty cares!
" 'Tis only love like ours attends
" When man unto the skies ascends.
" I wished to know thy secret vow;
" Among the stars I seek it now
" Where it is written—I shall see
" As clear as they thy honesty.
" I know I have been rash, and feel
" Thy grief for me is deep and real.
" Forgive me for the sake of love
" In every tear my grave above.
" I have no father, mother, brother;
" Thou wept my brother, father, mother,
" Thou wert my all—O Axel, swear
" In death that thou wilt hold me dear!
" Thou swearest—why should I deplore?
" The sweetest tale in all its lore
" Has life revealed to me. Thy maid,
" O may she on thy heart be laid,
" And may her ashes not repose
" Here in this land late won from foes?
" Lo, Axel, o'er the moon is cast

" A cloud ! ah, soon, when it has passed,
" Then shall I die, then glorified
" My shade shall sit the other side,
" Beseeching good for thee, and so
" With all heaven's eyes to look below.
" A foreign rose let grace my tomb,
" And when it dies in wintry gloom,
" The sun's child, muse upon her woe
" Who slumbers under northern snow.
" Her days of bloom they could not last—
" See, Axel, now the cloud is passed !
" Farewell, farewell ! "—she softly sighed,
Then gently pressed his hand and died.

From underground where the river flows,
Not Death, but his young brother rose,
Pale Madness, who is crownèd e'er
With poppies in his tangled hair,
Who now glares wildly at the skies,
Now earthward lets his glances slip,
With laughter round distorted lip,
And tears in half-extinguished eyes.
He lays his hand on Axel's brow,—
Ah, Axel wanders round her now
Entombed, as in old sagas went
Around his hoard a dead man's sprite ;

The sea-sands hear him day and night
In pitiful and dread lament:

"Be still, be still, thou sea, no more
"Must thou thus lash and beat the shore!
"Thou only dost disturb my dreams;
"I do not love thy many streams,
"Which sometimes froth in bloody tide—
"Thou bearest death unto my side.
"Here lately lay a youth and bled;
"I now strew roses on his tomb,
"For he was like—I well know whom—
"With her at spring-time I shall wed.
"They tell me earth has rocked to sleep
"My bride, and that the grass grows deep
"Upon her breast: love hath not died;
"She sat at night on the steep hill-side
"As pale as limners Death portray—
"But that was from the moon's white ray;
"Her lips and cheeks were frozen through—
"But that came when the north-wind blew;
"I bade the dear-loved one to stay—
"She stroked my brow in gentle way,
"For it was dark and heavy then,
"But soon became it light again.

" And in the far East rose before
" Me days, ah, days that are no more,
" Those azure days and passing fair—
" How happy they, poor Axel, were!
" A castle stood green woods among
" Whose towers unto her belong;
" I lay there wounded in the strife,
" And with a kiss she gave me life,
" And also gave her heart to me,
" So rich and warm a heart had she!
" Now in that withered breast at last
" It frozen lies—and all is past!
" Ye stars, that burn among the skies,
" I pray you vanish from my eyes!
" A morning star was known to me—
" It sunk down in a bloody sea.
" The scent of blood comes from the sand,
" And here is blood upon my hand!"—

So mourns he under Sotaskär.
When day enkindles he is there,
Nor goes he when the day is flown,
But sitteth there in ceaseless moan.
One morning dead beside the sea,

With hands composed in prayer, sat he,
And tears his pallid face had worn,
Half-frozen in the winds of morn;
Unto his true-love's barren tomb
His eyes were turned in misty gloom.

——o——

Such was the tale I heard of old.
How tenderly it then was told!
Though thirty winters' snows have been,
It still exists my heart within.
For with their features fixed and sharp,
The childhood scenes are pictured well
In souls of bards, where small they dwell
Like Aslög[11] in King Heimer's harp,
Until as she they forward press,
Betraying then their godliness,
With beauteous robes, with manners high
And golden hair and kingly eye.
In childhood's heaven are hung untold
Sweet lyres well-wrought in ruddy gold;
What man may write in aftertime,
As hero great, or flower small,
In visions fairer glided all
Before his eye in childhood's prime.

Still sometime when the quail doth sing
Melodiously in greening spring,
And moon comes from the eastern wave,
A spirit rising from the grave,
Painting the dale and mountain-head
With mournful colors of the dead,
Then are there rustlings in mine ear,
And then again I seem to hear
That olden tale, known far and wide,
Of Axel and his Russian bride.

NOTES TO AXEL.

NOTES TO AXEL.

1. The Carolinian Era is the time of Karl the Twelfth.

2. A bauta-stone is a monument to a dead warrior inscribed with runes.

3. Bender is a fortified town on the Dniester in Southern Russia, the retreat of Karl the Twelfth after the disastrous battle of Pultowa from 1709 to 1712.

4. Holofzin is a village in Poland where Karl the Twelfth attacked the Russians in 1708.

5. The royal body-guard was limited to seven or nine members, equal either to the stars in Charles' Wain or to the daughters of Mnemosyne, the muses.

6. Rolf Krake was a king of Denmark in prehistoric times, much lauded in northern sagas for his prowess in battle. When treacherously surrounded by conspirators under his half-sister Skuld, seeing all his comrades fallen, he with grim pleasure cleft helmet after helmet with his great sword, seeking "only company in death."

7. Pultowa is a walled city in Russia where Karl the Twelfth was defeated by Peter the Great in 1709.

8. Frans Michael Franzén was born in Finland in 1772. He and Bishop Tegnér and Archbishop Wallin form the brilliant triad of distinguished Swedish poets of that time. His lyrics are exceedingly popular in Finland and Sweden, and are particularly characterized by beauty of diction and sweetness of fancy.

9. Sigurd figures in northern sagas as chiefest of heroes. He slew the terrible dragon Fofnir and was surnamed Fofnisbane, or

Dragon-slayer, in commemoration of that exploit. He is represented as bearing a shield of ruddy gold on which was engraven a dragon, and Gram was the good sword with which he was girded. His noble horse was named Grane and was twelve feet high. They were inseparable companions, and when Sigurd was slain, Grane hung down his head in sorrow. Sigurd was the lover of the princess Brynhild, whose tower was encircled by enchanted fire, through which the hero rode to seek the fair maiden. Their passionate and mournful history is found in the ballads of the Elder Edda and in the Lay of the Niebelungen of a later day.—(See Prof. R. B. Anderson's *Norse Mythology* and Auber Forestier's *Echoes from Mist-Land.*)

10. Sotaskär is a rocky island among the numerous clusters of such in the vicinity of Stockholm. Leucas in Greece is famed as being the rock whence Sappho cast herself into the sea because of disappointment in love. The story of Hjalmar and Ingeborg is as follows:

Hjalmar and Odd were two renowned chieftains, and as subjects of King Ane the Old lived over eighteen centuries ago. Hjalmar loved Ingeborg, the daughter of the king, and his love was returned, but the king opposed their union for the reason that Hjalmar was not of royal lineage. Odd and Hjalmar were one day met at Sotaskär by their enemies, the twelve sons of Andgrim, mightiest among whom was Agantyr with the sword Tirfing. They two slew the twelve, yet when Odd turned to look for his companion who had fought Agantyr, he saw him leaning against a mound sorely wounded, and to his sad queries Hjalmar answered, "Every man must sometime die. Bear thou my farewell-song to Sweden." Thereupon he sang the famous death-song, which I in part translate:

* * * *

Fair the king's daughter
Followed beside me,
E'en to the islands
By Agnefit.

True was the tale she
Told unto me then,
That she should never
More me behold.

* * * *

Bear to the king's hall
Corselet and helmet.
Them before all thou
There shalt display.
Heave will the heart of
Her the king's daughter,
Seeing the corselet
Cut in the breast.

Free from my finger
The ruddy gold ring;
Go thou and give it
Young Ingeborg.
That will console her,
Soften her sorrow
That she shall never
More me behold.

* * * *

Thus died Hjalmar. Odd bore his body to the court of Ane the Old, placing it beside the door, and, entering with the helmet and coat of mail, laid them at the feet of the king saying, "Hjalmar is fallen." He then sought the presence of Ingeborg. She sat upon a stool weaving a mantle for her lover, and Odd approaching her said mournfully, "Hjalmar greeteth thee and sendeth thee this ring in his death moment." Ingeborg took the ring, looked at him, uttered no word, but sunk beside him under the spell of death. Odd thereupon bore her to the door of the court and laid her in Hjalmar's arms muttering, "Now shall they dead enjoy the bliss which fate denied them living." Hjalmar and Ingeborg were buried in the same mound at Sotaskär. Odd wandered far off into strange countries, and coming at length to Jerusalem, became a Christian. The tumulus existed many centuries, and it is related that the spirits of Hjalmar and Ingeborg still haunt the place.—(See Fryxell's *Sweden.*)

11. Aslög was the daughter of Sigurd and Brynhild. When King Heimer learned that her parents were dead and that Aslög too was in danger, procuring a large harp, he concealed within it the child together with the greater part of his riches, and in the guise of a beggar wandered to the far North, that he might thus avert disaster from the little one. He often freed her from confinement in the deep forest, when none was near, to allow her glimpses of the green wood and the grass and the blue sky, but replaced her on approaching the abode of men. One evening he arrived at a solitary hut among the mountains of Norway, where dwelled an old peasant and his wife, and, though inhospitably received, was given a place to rest. The woman, attracted by a rich fringe protruding from the harp and by a golden bracelet under his ragged sleeve, prevailed upon her husband to murder Heimer as he slept, whereupon the wicked deed was done. The harp was opened and Aslög came forth. She was taken, clad in the homespun garments of the people who now assumed her guardianship, and was known as Kraka the Shepherdess for a long time afterward. Subsequently she became the wife of King Ragnar, her beauty and intelligence having been made known to him by some of his subjects who were travelling in that portion of the country. For this and other beautiful northern legends, see Anderson's *Norse Mythology;* also for the names of Thor and Odin which are mentioned in AXEL.

Milton Keynes UK
Ingram Content Group UK Ltd.
UKHW040929180224
437992UK00003B/118

9 783385 331570